Fragmentations

By The Same Author

Razorblade

In the Mountain's Shadow

Fragmentations

Isabella Falconeri

Talon & Quill

TALON
&QUILL

The Inventor

We weren't the first. I still remember as a child the elders of our generation.

The Greats.

Great grandmothers and Great grandfathers. But we were close. We were so close to those beginnings we still had the stories of the Firsts.

The one whose spines began to straighten. Whose grunts became more than just guttural tones.

Those first communicators. The first to break from their brethren. To become different. To embrace it. To feel that spark of what you now call consciousness.

Being and unbeing.

Knowing.

It came slowly.

Internal dialogue, deliberation.

Conspiratorial collaboration.

Language for conveyance.

A beautiful, wondrous thing.

The ability, with sound, to form an idea into something almost tangible.

I believe it was language that became the cataclysm which allowed us to become what we are.

The process of stringing together sounds to make words to pass on thoughts from me to you.

The ultimate puzzle, language.

The essence of knowledge.

I always had a way with words.

I never knew their power.

Not until that day.

The Invention

On her knees she looked around the glade she knelt in…
the grass bending beneath her.

She felt the wind tickle the sweat beading at her neck.
She exhaled.

Deep breaths.

She took another long pull of oxygen and looked up at her captor.

Beyond him she saw a bird flying, conquering the air. Conquering
the element.

Tears welled in her eyes.

She brought her arms up, hands meeting near her heart. Palms flat
against one another and raised them like an arrow to the sky. All
fingers pointed at the bird in flight above her.

She willed her spirit to shoot from her fingertips… up,
away from this place.

She beseeched it.

"Go," she spoke.

That mix of people behind her, some silent, some wailing, others hurling insults. They all stilled to watch

her final moments. Heard that final word. Looked up as one, the bird no longer in sight.

Another breath.

The knife raised, ready to strike.

A boom echoed.

The ground began to shake.

The world trembled.

She took her chance.

She ran.

Ran past the stunned crowd. Amongst and beyond them/

The ground opening and swallowing up whatever it could.

All random.

As if a predator lay beneath the waves of turf prowling under

the surface, only rising when sure of a kill. Full of greed.

The people ran with her.

Those that could, those that were still able.

When they finally rested, the undulating earth had become newly calm as a windless sea.

Far away from the killing glade. They looked at her in awe. Came to touch her hair, to rest their hands on her shoulders.

One finally spoke.

"What happened?"

Others chimed in, murmuring, arguing amongst themselves.

"She spoke to something, and it answered," came a voice from the crowd.

"Go?" said one.

"No," said another, "God."

Cries of fear and confusion followed.

She had no idea what they were talking about. It came back in rush.

The bird.

Her command.

Go. She had willed it, but it had not happened. And these people now thought she was the cause of the rippling earth. That she had brought this upon them for their attempt on her life.

She flushed, she could use this to get away quickly as long as she played it right.

She hushed them. "Yes, that is correct. I spoke to God."

"Kneeling," she continued, "I beseeched him, and he answered me."

She waited a moment.

"He will bring destruction upon those who seek to harm me."

A survivor stepped forward, "begone from here, we do not want to incite the wrath of your protector."

Glad of her reprieve, she made hastily to leave, aware of how close she was to getting away.

A group of voices raised in protest as she turned away.

One was louder than the others, a frail woman with bruises smattering over her arms. A gleam of hope brightened her eyes, "where is he, who is he, and why does he protect you?"

Curiosity more than anger defining her features.

Another woman seeking the same type of protection the girl had claimed for herself. From the crowd came a few sneers, a few wary glances.

Fearing her ruse would not hold out long enough to grant her escape, she cast about in her mind.

How to make the lie stick and secure her safety... and maybe that of a few other victims in the crowd.

When she was young she had an imaginary friend. A small boy with the voice of an old man; he would tell her stories. It was from these cherished memories she drew inspiration.

"He does not always answer; he only does so when he chooses. But he is around us. In the trees, in the rocks, in the air. You cannot see him. He has no form, but he knows everything."

"He speaks to me. I am chosen," she stared meaningfully at the crowd before her. "I give him gifts. My friendship, adoration, compassion. I tell him everything. I ask his advice. He is like a father."

Looking straight into the eyes of the first woman, the hopeful one, she continued, "He is the father of everything and everyone; except those who are cruel and unkind–those He casts out until they have reformed."

The bruised woman fell to her knees, placed her hands flat against one another awkwardly and raised them towards the sky.

The crowd, seeing the woman act out the survivors' last

moments, fall to their knees as well; mimicking.

All ask for forgiveness and protection.

"Who is He to have such power?" One voice calls out in dissent.

"I do not know who He is," she answered, "it's not my place to question the father of everything, the maker."

The others nod emphatically. The downtrodden, the weak. All laying claim to a power of such magnitude it could make the ground shake. An easy devotion to justify.

She hid her smile behind her hair, head dipping in false modesty.

This could be very, very useful, she thought to herself.

The Parasite

I never wanted it.

He begged me.

Convinced me.

Broke me down.

Years, it took Him.

Until one day… I finally… gave in.

It torments me she thinks to herself.

It took so much from me.

My Body
My sense of self
My time
My youth
My job
My freedom
All my freedom.

My thoughts.

So much time dedicated to its wellbeing.

So much time dedicated to keep it alive.

And I've done it.

I've done it for Him.

He promised me.

He promised He'd help. Be a partner. Share the weight.

I should've known better.

This…progeny…was what He wanted.

It was what He was told he needed to round out His life.

His legacy.

His pride and joy.

And what did He do?

And what has He done?

No contribution and yet He shows it off like He should be praised for its goodness.

He loves this thing…this parasite.

I did too… once.

When it signified what we had built.

When it was the symbol representing our life, our partnership, our love.

And then… He cheated.

And He didn't just cheat.

He left.

And He didn't just leave.

He left for a younger, more malleable version of me.

And it wasn't just that He left… He… humiliated me.

He told me He loved me, asked me to reaffirm my devotion to Him, and then, the very next morning…

He was gone.

Vanished.

No note.

He didn't even bother.

I was so clueless I'd ended up calling the police.

The mockery-mixed-sympathy in their eyes was…

unendurable.

And after He'd left me, and I'd cried, and I'd begged.

He ignored me.

For years I've spent of myself… giving and giving and giving.

And after 3 months…

He finally called.

He'd been on a boat.

Not a boar, a yacht.

With her.

Enjoying the sunshine.

Getting color.

And His first words to me after 8 years and 3 months were

…"How is my son?"

And in that moment, I understood.

His intention was for me to spend the rest of my life rearing His child.

After having spent the majority of my youth rearing Him.

And He would spend the remainder of His year free...

Joyous.

Empty of responsibility.

Expecting me to bear all burdens, all obligations.

Leeching from my life-force to feed His.

And in that very same moment, I knew what I would do.

I would take something precious from Him...

Just as He had taken from me.

And in that moment of theft... Release.

Release from the responsibilities, ties, burdens.

In one...fell...swoop.

I knew, in the moment of my decision, that I would need to

execute my plan carefully.

In order not to lose my freedom the moment I gained it.

And so I began my plan.

Accidents happen all the time.

The Game

The game had barely started when a small child darted onto the field–a disruption rare enough to make even the oldest spectators shift uneasily.

Rensen saw the child and, for just a moment, the game fell away.

The crowd, the rules, the consequences– all background noise to that instinct to protect.

Rensen grabbed him, both of them falling to the ground in a singular movement. The grab just barely keeping the boy from the harm farther along.

As they hit the ground, a small notebook slipped from his pocket.

Liana, sharp-eyed and swift, snatched it up and began to read aloud.

Meanwhile, the play in the middle of the field had already begun and ended. Torus, captain of the opposing team, had been tackled to the ground.

Torus lay stunned, blinking up at the blue sky above.

Marcus and Tenny, inseparable since birth, were nearly perfect copies of one another.

Their mothers had been best friends since childhood; the pattern repeated.

Marcus, the boy, and Tenny, the girl.

They had just managed a spectacular play culminating in the prone form of Torus.

Satisfaction played over their features--until Liana's voice rang out, mocking--reciting the secret plays they'd spent months perfecting with Rensen.

They didn't run. Liana's speed was legendary--by the time they got there, the damage would be done.

They shared a glance.

Tenny flopped down beside Torus, plucking a blade of grass to twirl between her fingers.

Her feet kicked lazily behind her.

"Really," she sighed, blowing on the blade.

"You'd think your team had more integrity than this."

Torus blinked, eyes finally focusing on her face.

"If we'd known you planned to cheat, we wouldn't have bothered showing up," Marcus said, mirroring Tenny's pose on Torus's other side.

Marcus turned to Tenny, "Perhaps we should forego the whole thing and just leave now, what do you think?"

She matched his solemn tone.

"I think it just might be the best option." She began to rise, brushing grass from her knees.

"Liana!" shouted Torus, "stop that damn rambling and give it back."

His eyes close tiredly as her voice drones on. "Right. Now."

His final command carries across the field and her words cease as quickly as a snipped thread.

"You two--Up." He lifts his hands, palms open.

The twins grinned, jumped to help and hoisted him up together.

If your secrets are so fragile, maybe you shouldn't scribble them down where just anyone can find them," Liana sneers as she angrily tosses the book at Rensen and returns to her starting position.

From somewhere, applause echoed—too distant to place.

The game begins anew.

The War Dead

I was in the midst of a firefight.

It's such a unique experience to us.

We the warmongers and our victims.

I was hanging out of the airlock trying to grab ahold of Geraint's hand and pull him to safety.

I thought I was invincible.

Did you know that bullets don't fly straight?

So, for example, say you're hiding behind a big log, big enough of a trunk to hide you fully sitting up straight.

You know those logs, the ones that have fallen recently and are just pure bulk.

You're safe, right?

    Seems legitimate.

        Well, guess what?

            G

                r

                    a

                      v

                          i

                            t

                                y

Gravity takes those tiny little death dealing projectiles and

weighs 'em down.

So you think you're in the clear, right?

    But, their path is parabolic, especially over long distances.

        You know what that means?

You could be hiding, comfortable, behind that big old log of yours
and BAM!

        Whatchadoodle doo, what are you?

You're dead, that's what.

Knowing about that parabolic arc, knowing about how the wind can blow your bullet off course, those things.

Those things will make you a great sniper.

Anywho, I managed to grab onto Geraint fine, under full cover and everything.

But it wasn't my day, and that damn parabola socked it to me.

Socked it right into my liver.

Weird, wonderful thing about adrenaline is that you kinda don't even feel it.

And that's what keeps you going.

That's what protects that supremely powerful but equally fragile meatball brain of yours from deconstructing.

At least at first.

Then the pain hits.

Actually the pain gets worse once you get to the medic, from my limited experience.

It pays to stay the fuck away from the medic.

The damage those fellas do trying to fix you is almost as bad as the initial injury.

Did you know that 92% of medics are sadistic sociopaths?

Neither did I, I'm guessing, don't quote me.

The number has got to be more than 0; if you've ever met a medic in a time of need, you'd agree with me.

I'm not saying they're not actually getting you back up in tip top, I'm just saying… well, I guess I'm just saying, that's all.

    Well, there I am, my liquids pouring out of me just like that damnable leak in our barracks.

        Drip, drip.

Geraint's on, if you cared.

        I certainly didn't by that point.

But, because someone on this bird (couldn'ta been me, I swear it) musta pissed someone off…

        the ole bird gets hit too.

Right in 'er go juice.

        And kabluey, away we go.

        Fire, fire, burning bright amirite?

[intermission, cue the muzak]

So there I am, dead.

As well as the rest of us.

I don't remember squat.

I just know what I told you.

But then, from the dark, bleak, grey nothingness.

I... awaken.

My old platoon buddy Bill and I are standing right outside our homes.

No, not the barracks.

Our houses, I mean.

I don't know how they're next door to one another, considering he's out in Texas and I'm up in Montana.

And this sure as shit isn't my street.

But that sure as shit is my house.

Some guy with a bullhorn at the end of the row is shouting at us all.

"You have. 15 minutes to go into your homes. The

boxes to your right are for you. Take only what you

can fit in those boxes. Take anything you like, as long

as it's in the box. The box comes with you.

Everything else stays. You will meet me in 14

minutes and thirty eight seconds at the transport

behind me. Your timer, as you should be aware, has

already started. If you are not on the transport

before the provided time, you will be left behind."

By the time I heard fourteen, I'd already started to pony up.

I knew the game.

He wasn't original.

I'm trying to quickly deduce what would be the most advantageous to bring given I've got little to no information.

I come up with the following: cash, candy, cigarettes, and coffee beans. The four c's of continuance (or survivability).

I try to live my life under the guise of, if I would go for it in the event of a fire, I should probably find out how to disengage myself from it; I like to call those typa things Fire Hazards.

Needing things is not a good idea. Enjoying and experiencing is highly suggested. But the moment you need something, you're at a disadvantage. The best part of all four c's is that I do not need nor indulge in any of them, but there are many, many folks who do. This puts me in a unique situation in which I can provide those necessities to others and reap whatever I like. My supply is not likely to be diminished by my own cravings and I can choose to distribute when it suits me best.

Favors are wonderful, magical things.

Favors can't go up in smoke… unless the owe-er is dead. But seeing as I'm here, I'm thinking I got a lot of unspent favors from a lot of un-dead folk coming due.

I bet you're wondering if I've ever been in a fire.

No I have not, but I have seen them on tv and I considered it.

I'm one of the first on the transport meaning I get to choose my preferred seat. Middle is best.

Not first, not last. Slightly indistinguishable but directly next to this handy dandy emergency exit.

Bill comes shortly afterwards and sits next to me.

"What'd you bring," he asks.

Now, I'm not a fan of showing my wares to anyone and Bill here knows that.

So I embellish.

"Some plush socks, a fuzzy robe, and bubble bath," I say.

"How about you Bill?"

Bill opens his box in response.

It's a black lab puppy.

"Jesus Christ, I'm jealous Bill," I can honestly say I'm not joking, "what's its name?"

"Jillian," he says with a smirk and some tears well up in his eyes.

Bill has always been a softy. I get it though, that there is one sweet puppy. I briefly consider calling in one of the favors Bill owes me, but I want to see where this goes first.

That and, Jillian is most assuredly a Fire Hazard.

They fly us out to an abandoned airfield.

We pile out as ordered, each of us heaving these big damn boxes.

There's a grid of empty body bags laid out. We're instructed to set our boxes at the foot of our chosen body bags and get ready to be zipped.

Somebody tries to run.

I don't see who. But the minute they pass out of a 100 meter radius from the man with the bullhorn, they drop like a sack of potatoes. No movement can be seen, but their skin pallor immediately turns the green-grey of someone long dead.

"I don't have to tell you this, but if you wanted to leave you can, however leaving means finishing what's been done already", the man with the megaphone looks around pointedly.

"There's no shame in it," says the megaphone man, "but you will not get a second chance."

We all hurriedly zip ourselves in like we've been told.

I've never been one to shy away from being volun-told.

Once we're all in a hose gets fixed up to an aperture in the bag and we all go nighty night.

I come to as I hear others waking, I sit up and unzip myself.

We're on a different transport.

The loading bay of what looks like it must be a very large ship.

I grab my box and follow the blinking lights to the ramp of yet another, smaller ship.

Shit if this is purgatory, I can't imagine hell.

Transport to transport.

I wonder if we're either trying to confuse our scent or if getting to where we're going is just purely that difficult.

As I load my box under my seat and strap myself in, I start thinking about my life up to this point.

The people I still got things to say to.

I'm thinking about my family. My 2 month old niece and how, as she grows older, her mother will be talking to her about this person she's never met before.

I sure should have visited more.

Kinda crazy, strangers inundating a young kid's life like that. I wonder how she'll envision me; with the picture my sister paints.

My neighbor this time isn't Bill, it's a friendly lady named Gail.

Gail, while friendly, is freaking out.

It's odd how some people can just take weirdness and keep trucking on as if it were just any other old day. And then there's some people who realize the absurdity of it all and they just snap. Like those climate folks. There are so many of them, they been clamoring for years. It's surely happening. But the majority of us "truckers' just trudge along.

Knowing but not doing nothing.

It's not like we aren't aware.

We're just wired differently.

We adapt.

It will likely cause more pain later but for now, if it's less troublesome, we'd just as likely continue on taking the air and taking it easy.

Probably some fucked up mutated survival mechanism.

Looks like one of the bodybaggers didn't get on the ship in time. She's running along like she'll make it; banging on the side of the transport like its a city bus.

Well that surely puts Gail over the edge and she starts hammering on the window with her fist.

I shout over the noise of the engines, "you know that young'n ma'am?"

Gail looks at me wild-eyed, her hair coming out in tendrils bit by bit, "Heavens no, I would just want someone to try for me, dammit."

That's a fair point.

I incline my head, put her out of the way and pull the emergency door handle.

The wind whips me against the side of the ship but I take the hit. Something's got me in the gut, it's painful, but I keep going and throw out a hand.

We clasp and I start to pull her in when I look up in terrible realization, "shit, I've been here before."

The young woman is in, but then something hits the transport in her go-juice.

"God DAMMIT," I say, as the blast hits me.

Alaska

A group of people are backpacking on a cold snowy Alaskan night.

They came across what seemed like a small outpost, looming in the darkness.

Cold and excited for a civil meal, they went inside.

It was a bar, with an old jaundiced library lining the back wall.

Two bartenders manned the building alone; no other patrons in sight.

They greeted the newcomers and invited them in to warm themselves by the fire.

The group ordered drinks, chatting amicably.

One of the girls in the group, Kellan, mentioned she always

assumed books on display were just for show—not for reading.

A bartender, slightly offended, offered her one of his favorites.

Its cracked spine and dog-eared pages glowed in the firelight.

"These are read," he told her, 'and read often."

He tapped the cover with his forefinger,"—especially this one."

Before she could ask more, the group decided to move on, wanting to make camp before dark.

The bartenders asked if the group would like to stay the night—there were rooms available.

The group agreed, delighted. They were led back outside, into the unpierced night.

A solitary lamp lit against the cold bobbed along in front of them.
The group huddled together, staggering when the wind blew too hard against their insufficient winter gear.

They arrived at a small cabin next door.

The bartender showed them in, then left quickly.

They were so tired they barely looked around, in their minds, the cabin was a significant improvement from the sinister outdoors.

Back in the bar, the bartender stomped his wet boots and wiped them aggressively on the mat.

He and his colleague avoided each other's eyes.

The one behind the bar commented, "maybe they'll survive," with a casual shrug of his shoulders.

The other shot him a look. "I wouldn't count on it."

Back in the cabin, the group fractures into their separate beds.

One of the boys slipped into Kellan's room, easing under her blankets to steal a kiss, but, exhausted and unmoved she tossed him out with a curt, "get lost."

Annoyed, she opened the unnamed book from the bar, immediately engrossed in its contents.

Across the hall, another member of the group opened his closet.

A few garments from former tenants hung there, forgotten. He barely registered them before undressing and settling in for the night.

Kellan stayed up late while the others fell asleep.

Reading late into the night, well past when she should have been asleep.

Sleep, though, eventually claims her too.

She is unexpectedly awoken by one of the girls moaning in the other room.

The book fell from her chest when she jolted out of bed.

She listened for a moment, trying to distinguish the sentiment of the moans; unable to determine, she decided to check in, regardless of what she might interrupt.

As she entered the hallway, her steps creaked; the noise startled her.

She looks left and right, the doors seemingly endless.

There.

Josephine's room.

She opened the door slowly, "Josephine?"

Josephine jerked up from the bed, "Kellan!"

She pulled her knees to her chest and cried harder.

Kellan closed the door softly behind her and went to her bedside, rubbing Josephine's shoulders, unsure of herself.

Kellan wrapped her in a hug.

Josephine leaned into it but didn't speak.

Kellan probed gently, until Josephine finally answered.

"I was attacked… by a fawn," Josephine said, embarrassed.

"I know it sounds insane. I must have been dreaming. But it felt so real. I've never experienced anything like it."

Josephine looked into her friend's eyes, desperate for something other than disbelief.

Kellan simply comforted her and insisted it was just a nightmare. They agreed Kellan would sleep with Josephine for the rest of the night.

The next morning, Kellan woke up alone.

Josephine's pillow bore a note.

We tried to wake you. We're going ahead.

Meet us at the forest's edge a few miles up the trail.

Kellan muttered curses under her breath as she got ready, furious at being left behind.

Grumbling, she began checking the cabin to make sure no one had left anything behind.

Each room's closet still held clothes.

She threw up her hands, "I have to do everything for these people," she muttered angrily.

She quickly packed the forgotten items.

She made her way to the laundry room--finding still more clothing.

All different sizes.

I didn't check sizes, she thought wonderingly, maybe these aren't ours.

She hesitated, considering whether to unpack everything.

Then she heard a noise.

Behind the laundry baskets, a wooden door with an iron bolt stood ajar.

Curious, she crawled through.

The door led to a large bathroom. A faucet dripped wastefully.

Drip. Drip. Drip.

She tried the handle — locked.

A flicker of light caught her eye. Across the room, another door stood open, leading to a living room.

Kellan, entranced, walked through.

Inside, a small television buzzed with white noise. Two elderly Swedes sat in silence, bathed in its static light. Neither turned to acknowledge her.

She hesitated, but felt drawn in.

She moved in front of the screen.

Their eyes were oily white and they were both in aged, saggy underwear, yellowed with sweat and age.

The man sat in a dark stain on the couch.

 Brown-red. Old blood. The stain easily visible between his widely spread thighs. Her gaze drifted to the woman, rocking slowly in time, metronome-steady.

Kellan's mouth opened in horror. The man tilted his head toward Kellan. The woman spoke, voice placid, thick with a Swedish accent."Vouldn't you please gif us a tour of the 'otel?"

The stench from the woman's mouth is nearly tangible. A viscous cloud of olive green aerosolized mucus and stained teeth.

Kellan's trance shattered. Her heart raced. She turned and fled. She slammed the door closed in embarrassed alarm. She felt like a child running up the stairs of the cellar after the light has been turned off.

Noticing a bolt, she locked the door and backed away. The wooden door she'd entered through now led somewhere else. Lost, she wandered through doors and rooms until she found herself in an industrial kitchen — all chrome and gleaming surfaces.

"I must be dreaming," she muttered. Then screamed it. The sound dampened by the thick walls.

A door slammed open. A man appeared, startled by her presence. Cookie tins lined the shelves behind him. The air smelled of fresh-baked sweets. Kellan stepped back quickly, saying the first thing that came to her mind, "I was trying to find the bathroom."

The man's suspicious look threw her off guard.

He scoffed, grabbed a cookie, shoved it into his mouth. Crumbs lining his lips. "Mmm," he moaned, eyes fluttering, "so good."

She eyed a cookie covered in colorful chocolate, aware she hadn't all morning. She made a reflexive move toward it, tempted--but the man's glare stopped her in her tracks.

Not for you, his look said.

He turned and hissed over his shoulder, "come with me."

She followed him.

He leads her into the cool morning air.

Finally out, she takes a deep breath of the outside air, hesitating on the threshold. She looks around herself, confused.

Last night, everything was covered under snowdrifts, this morning, unbelievably, it's Spring and everything has become green and verdant.

A small outdoor cafe lines this side of the building. People sit at bistro tables in the grass, eating quietly.

Kellan wanders among them, stunned. As she passes, unbeknownst to her, all the diner's attention turns, one by one, their focus on her. Their heads moving in unison.

A shrill cry for help cuts through the morning air.

Only Kellan reacts.

Josephine runs towards them from a short distance waving her arms and crying. "Please help! Please!" she shouts. "They hurt my friend!"

Kellan runs towards her. Josephine, breathless, collapses into her arms sobbing.

Behind them, the diners all stand and begin walking towards the girls.

Calm.

Unified.

Their eyes hollow.

Kellan glances up, then back at Josephine who has not yet noticed.

She shakes her, "look."

Josephine turns, jerking in Kellan's arms as she sees the oncoming crowd. "What are you doing? Help us!"

Kellan takes only a second to decide, knowing they need to run.

She begins to back away slowly, step by step.

The group follows them, intent.

As she takes her last backward step, she feels a falling sensation.

A shadow passes over their heads.

Kellan looks up. Their steps have taken them under the shadow of a wide copper arbor.

The diners stop at the edge of the shadow.

Gathering in the light.

None cross.

They wait in deafening silence, watching.

Kellan tries to move — but can't.

She stands frozen, blood rushing past her ears.

She hears a heavy step behind her.

The Grower

I have a gift.

Before the fires, before the destruction, my gift was a curse. I was ostracized from my community. I was alone. No one would come near me. Mothers would pull their children from my path.

I barely left the confines of my own home.

And then… everything changed.

My gift?

Growing.

I didn't realize the benefits of my gift until after the End.

I was one of the few people lucky (or unlucky) enough to survive the deluge.

I wandered aimlessly for a long time; starving.

Starvation.

It was only then that I truly understood the extent of my gift.

While everything else remains barren, I can grow.

The crops are waiting, ready to be harvested.

The first step is to make a small hole, the smaller the better.

No sharp tools, just fingers.

Fingers to loosen the area slowly, wrap a finger or two around it and pull.

Sometimes it comes out in pieces, but it's best to get it whole.

In order to ensure continued production, you've got to seam up the edges as best you can.

I whisper to them sometimes, I think they can hear me.

"Grow," I tell them, "grow."

I met my wife sometime later.

She was orphaned after the End; all alone.

Like me.

We startled one another scavenging amongst the rubble. I showed her my gift. It took her a while to come around, but once she acknowledged the benefits of my gift, she was easily persuaded.

I'm a good provider and I love her dearly.

She's become a master chef. The things she can whip up with my crop.

She's learned to help me cultivate too.

She's better than I am at mending once we've harvested.

You can barely tell there was ever a hole by the time she's finished.

We had our first child last year. He's been blessed with my gift. He will be able to thrive where others cannot, provide where others cannot.

He will have to be strong and brave, to ensure his gift is never used without his permission.

I stand here, with my wife and child at my side, looking down over our settlement. The life we've made.

Old scars overlap new ones.

The old and new stitches crosshatch over my skin.

My body continues to grow these tumors, providing us with a renewable source of sustenance and life.

I am the Grower.

The Story of Death

On the day prior, the Mother and her son, the Monster, had been in the countryside having a picnic.

In the sun dappled meadow they lay, decadence strewn amongst them.

Having just finished their coupling, the Mother, fondly wiping her son's brow, states, "it's time to try again."

The next evening the Maiden exits her patrons carriage before the ball.

Her white gloves, red lips on display.

The elder gentleman, her patron, kissing her upraised hand, leads her to the foyer to be announced.

They dance exuberantly, unaware.

Later, the Mother requests their presence, just the two of them, in her parlor.

She plies them with drinks, but they need no encouragement.

The drinks take their toll, the patron and the Maiden are led to an upstairs bedroom.

The Mother and the Monster watch, unencumbered.

The Monster, catching glimpses of the Maidens smooth white breasts as they rise and fall with each movement, feels anticipation.

They are led willingly, easy and pliant.

The Mother leads the patron to the uppermost level.

The patron moves behind her, lost in lust, while she braces herself against the gallery rail, eyes gleaming as she watches the spectacle unfold beneath them.

The Monster appears, all charm.

His handsome features more prominent in the soft light.

The Maiden, initially unsure, begins to waver.

She softly acquiesces and they begin.

It's gentle at first, but only at first.

Then it becomes violent.

So violent, she begins to scream.

Unable to escape, she falls limp, tears streaking her face.

The Mother watches calmly; the patron oblivious.

Later, the Maiden lay upon the floor, dress torn, weeping.

The Monster gently stroking her face, wiping her tears.

The Maiden happens to look up.

She sees the patron, his throat slit.

The Mother watches her calmly, hands bloodied.

The Maiden begins to scream again; her mouth is covered by the

Monsters hand; restrained.

Her legs beating a staccato on the floor.

Her eyes widen, the tone of her screams change.

Her belly begins to grow.

And grow.

And grow.

Suddenly sharp pains begin; cramping.

The Monster has backed away, watching.

The Maiden cries for help.

The newly born baby writhes under its caul.

The Maiden snatches up the child and cradles it to her chest.

Terrified, bewildered, she names it what she wishes for herself.

Death.

The Mother stalks away into the darkness of a corridor, humming happily.

The Monster cradles them both to his chest and carries them away.

A month later, Death is a toddler and the Maiden has aged.

She has recovered, and has decided to run.

She intends to take Death with her.

The Maiden and Death smuggle themselves out.

They wait at the train station.

The foggy, dewy morning barely resolved itself around them.

The horn blows and they ascend.

The Maiden manages to run for almost a decade.

But the Mother and the Monster do not give up.

They are never far behind.

For they know that if the Maiden does not love the Monster.

Death will be the end of them.

But they underestimate the Maiden.

Death ages quickly, as does the Maiden.

The Maiden loves Death.

Death loves the Maiden.

Caught, finally, the Maiden, now a Crone, perishes in the Mothers grasp.

The Maiden would not yield.

Death felt the Maiden go.

Death committed herself to her name.

Death wielded death, and when she was done, the Mother and the Monster were no more.

Death needed life to survive.

Death needed life to thrive.

This is the story of Death.

Body Double

Every morning I wake up, I transfer to today's body.

Every night before I go to sleep, I prepare tomorrow's body.

When the morning comes, I shove yesterday's body into the bin marked "Old Body" and forget about it.

I've never really considered what happened to yesterday's body.

I've never had to.

Until today.

When I woke today, all was different.

They had visited. They always do.

But they've never historically accomplished anything.

Until today.

I should have taken more precautions. I had no idea they were so
... invested in my destruction.

They must've been studying me for a long time to conceive of
this plan.

I woke ready to begin the laborious body exchange.

But not today.

Today's body has been destroyed.

The devastation was, um, extensive.

To be perfectly honest, I was shocked.

I've never considered what I would do in this situation.

In fact, I've become so used to this routine I haven't considered much at all.

So today... this morning... in this wake... well, I... I fear I didn't do much of anything except gape for probably far too long.

Whilst I am in today's body, I am indestructible.

They've tried damaging me that way before.

See the trouble is, it takes a full day to grow today's body.

And today's body cannot be borne, or rather... worn.

So here I am...

...gaping at my body whilst in a body meant for the bin and no way with which to grow a new body.

After casting about for what to do, I feel I am at a loss.

So I sit down and consider the problem further.

The only problem is, my fingers have begun a small tremor, and in my contemplation, I failed to notice my tongue and managed to nick it with my teeth.

It has yet to stop bleeding.

This copper metallic taste in my mouth has ruined my thought process entirely and I am ready to do something desperate.

I search the small room for an answer but there is only: bed, body, bin.

So I pull the tab for the "Old Body" bin and squeeze myself in.

The box closes.

All the air sucks out.

The walls become gelatinous and I begin to feel a tingling

sensation where yesterday's body and gelatin connect.

I use my trembling hands to try to push it away but the skin starts to tear.

I push against the back side of the bin, knees to chest, until I break the mechanism and am released.

I tear away where the rest of my body is still stuck to goo.

Well, there goes my beauty, I think to myself sardonically as I check the wounds.

I bandage the open wounds with sheets.

Considering the futility of that exercise, I return to sitting and meditating.

However it doesn't take long until the badges are saturated with unstaunched blood.

It doesn't seem like there's much else I can do.

So I proceed about the rest of my day as if I had today's body.

Each minute, each hour more aches, pains, tremors.

I feel my body dying all around me as the day progresses.

Wow, I think to myself when I feel my cognition slipping, what a way to go.

Meat Machine

"The process is quite difficult to get right.

It's taken me eons to perfect.

It's… kinetic.

Matter of fact, it's… Life

I've spent my entire life completing it. The detritus of a life full lived.

Our kind thrives on work such as this, but no one else has yet succeeded. There's self propulsion, propagation, population.

But nothing like this.

It's hard to describe my work.

In layman's terms, I mean.

It's taken so long to get it right.

Even the fluidity of its movements.

Joints, articulation, locomotion.

Fragility.

The prototypes after all this time.

At this point they seem downright ghastly but at each progressive
step, more knowledge, more capacity.

You've no idea the lack of literature regarding this subject,
you'd be shocked.

It's been entirely trial and error.

I had to be very conscious about which choices I wanted to make about its development.

For instance, I never intended for it to be indestructible.

I always wanted its ephemeral qualities to be apart of its nature.

Our longevity inhibits our sense of urgency.

I think it's a failing of our species and I wanted to curb it in theirs.

The component, though. Understanding what was needed.

That was the key.

That was what took so long. So many interconnected cogs, all requiring synchronization to fulfill their purpose.

Two balloons which inflate with intake.

Four chambers which propel action and inaction.

Thump…thump… thump…thump.

The mechanism which powers the machine.

A central computer too, one which powers cognition, capacity.

Nothing near the fragmentation we're capable of but…
primitive.

Articulation took many twists and turns.

Apologies, I've told this story many times and I find myself falling
into a cadence.

One which amuses me, but no others, at least not those who
have heard it more than once.

But there's always the newly curious, those interested in
science, in perpetuating the study.

I'm old now, and I've accomplished that which I set out to do so many lifetimes ago.

They're new to the study, they want to take it further, on other worlds.

But I am fulfilled with my creation, and the duplication it generates.

This beings capacity never ceases to amaze me.

Even now, in its newly premature capability.

These are the first, but, to me they represent the inexplicable, the indomitable, the irreplaceable honor of being the catalyst; I sense its untapped potential.

These are the first, but, to me they represent the inexplicable, the indomitable, the irreplaceable honor of being the catalyst; I sense its untapped potential.

There are of course some poorly developed individual cases but, to my mind, wiping those would be detrimental to the experiment. If I'm not able to see the outcome without intervention, I cannot call myself a scientist.

So I wait, and I watch.

But the mechanism, you see, that's the beauty.

Think of these separate parts.

Balloons, elastic string, meat, stiff rods for stability.

Transforms into a walking, talking, thinking being.

I've been told my hubris knows no bounds with regards to my creation.

My, so fondly called by my detractors, Meat Machine.

I call it Human.

The Ranger

I've never seen anything as scary as that little girl.

As a cop, I've seen more horrible shit than your average human.

That's not saying much — from what I've seen there's a lot of people seen an awful lot of awful shit.

Me though, I got theirs plus mine, plus more.

The rites of the job.

But... there's... I dunno... rules? standards?

I don't know what happened to make that kid the way she was
but...

You know how people say nurture and all that gunk?

Like, this kid? She... she didn't have enough time on earth to
garner that much evil.

                   That shit takes time.

     Eons maybe.

          She didn't come out blank though; not her.

She must've come out wrong.

No, not wrong. I seen those that come out wrong.

                   That kid.

There aren't words for what she became.

I read something once… something about how women have more range than men.

They love harder.

They rage harder.

Their wells go deeper.

Maybe it's because they exist in a perpetually wounded state.

Maybe it's because they have to have more of everything in order to make life.

Who knows.

All I know is…

I have never seen anything as scary as that little girl.

Kodokushi

The voices come and go.

They tell me things.

The act of acknowledgment is necessary for the body to release its grip on the thing we all call soul.

Acknowledgment of death.

It has to be seen.

It has to be perceived.

By one of my own.

So they wait.

They discuss in my hearing.

Their voices strange and inhuman.

"If she's not found soon she'll rival Benny's last waster," voice one.

"Hot Damn! Benny has had the longest streak in a while, I can't wait," voice two.

"When was the longest?" voice three.

"Longest waster?" voice two.

"About eight years in recent times," voice one pauses, "things have changed," he adds sullenly, "old days, it could be centuries, there's some as yet still undiscovered."

How long do you think you could withstand the constant

burrowing.

The tracks laid lightly by flies.

Paralyzed

Stuck

I would give my right arm just to be able to blink.

Not that it functions much nowadays anyhow.

You know… once the panic ebbs… well that does take quite a while… but once it ebbs…

Really all that's left is pain.

Well pain and cloudy awareness.

I don't even know whether or not I'm truly dead yet or if these are just phantom feelings.

Like the pain you get in a lost limb.

Or if I'm in a separate place.

A holding place.

That's what the voices say.

Alone

Every once in a while.

They don't come all that often.

But then again, the shadows do… and I'm not sure about the shadows.

But the shadows definitely don't talk.

The things you see out of the corner of your eyes while you're up… alive.

They love to play tricks when you're unable to glance in their direction.

I feel things.

Things tugging at my toes.

Nibbling at my fingertips.

Like when you go into cold dark water and the fish begin to get curious.

I hear things too.. not just the voices.

The slap stick swish of bare feet across the ground

I try to call out but no sound comes. They're less concerned when they know I can't catch them with my living reflexes.

The house creaks comfortingly.

The sink drips.

The tick tick tick of the clock.

The outside noises ebb and flow.

The mailman shoves the mail through the door slot.

It piles and slides gently. I try to strain my eyes to read.

Something to ease the loneliness. The boredom.

.I watch the sunlight creep its way across the floor.

I tried counting it once. I got past a month and experienced such tremendous terror I decided it was better not to know.

Day in.

Day out.

I feel my insides pooling outward.

The disintegrating descent.

Pine and Flesh

Nighttime, though, that's the worst.

More bugs. More than bugs.

And still I wait.

Undiscovered.

The Vagrant

We found her ID outside our building.

Walking up.

We'd been out for supplies.

First time in a long time that a supply run had gone so smoothly.

It was a weird thing to drop.

She'd been my roommate before it all happened.

And we just never split up after.

We found the others, holed up in this building. We just let the world burn itself to ashes.

She was the last vestige of my old life.

We clung to one another.

It helped make it reality.

Helped prevent it from becoming nothing... disappearing in the
smoke and ash of each long, dark, suffering day.

We found her ID outside our building.

I felt hope.

I rushed inside.

I didn't hear anything.

Our building was like one of those old hotels with a hole in the
center and a balconied mezzanine on each floor.

So you could look out, down in the main plaza, see all your

neighbors.

The paranoids dream.

The primary reason we survived.

We could see.

We could watch.

It's black maw, mocking.

I rushed up to the third floor, ran inside, heedless

of the danger.

Calling her name.

No answer.

I ran back outside to the mezzanine.

The railing hitting my hip as I looked out at the others on the main floor.

"Do you see her?" I asked frantically.

One of the girls gasped and pointed.

I swung around in fright.

And there she was.

Standing behind me.

Sick.

Her face.

Her once beautiful face.

Ravaged by the disease.

It eats so quickly.

The pain and the anguish causes a sort of aphasia.

The seizing of emotions: each one a flicker: rage, anger, mania.

They're so dangerous.

They're so deranged.

They're so goddamn contagious.

I reach for her.

It's so horrible.

Then she snarls, lunging at me.

I grab her by the front of her shirt and thrust.

She topples over the railing.

Yowling like a car until the sound of the kick crunch of her body can be heard as it flattens on the floorboards below.

I turn away from the gruesome sight.

Tomorrow we will venture out again.

Zoetrope

Zoe is not a normal woman.

Zoe exists in the plural.

She is not one, but many.

There are four of her.

She… Flickers.

It's difficult, going through your day and:

Your arm becomes an inch shorter

Your teeth transform inside your mouth

Your breasts weigh heavy, and then they don't.

She's had to abstain from many things in her life.

Exercising, operating heavy machinery, stairs.

Stairs exist solely to plague her.

She is… compulsive… about men.

They are drawn to her.

She can't tell if its her constant damsel in distress existence

Or some other, darker reason

It works for her, though

It makes it easier for her

They're so helpful

and they taste so good.

Sometimes, she develops a crush

And she savors them a little longer.

                    That's how she feels about him

He's lasted so long

        She really likes him

            He makes her nervous

                    And when she's nervous

Her flickering gets more pronounced

    Flick, Jenna, Flick, Jamie, Flick, Beatrice, Flick, Rachel.

They don't actually have names, though.

        She would never be so gauche as to name them.

Thought they exist as separate beings

        They are also… intertwined with one another

The crush she has is dwindling, though

A new player has entered

A man

Lucas

And Lucas is already hooked

And so, with some small semblance of regret, she finishes off the last of her crush.

His whimpers, so tantalizing.

But she doesn't eat more than one meal at a time.

Out of respect, of course.

Each deserves her full... attention.

Reflections of a Post War Gladiator

There was a long time ago.

Back in old San Francisco.

The post-tech, prewar San Francisco.

With its... identity crisis.

It's uber wealthy, it's uber snobbish broken bubble.

I was walking.

I don't know where... probably a haircut.

When, in front of me, at a bus stop populated

with all manner of 'ciscan citizens.

A man.

A shirtless man... raving.

Raving under the awning of the bus stop shelter.

I don't believe he was raving about anything in particular.

I especially believe his ravings were not entirely in English or any language spoken by any other excepting himself.

I remember doing calculations.

I couldn't squeeze myself behind the stop as it nearly abutted the building behind it.

And, of the random personages scattered about awaiting the bus' arrival none were with him in the shelter and all stood in an errant semi circle of half aware distance from him.

Almost like a tentative crowd at a rock show.

The few feet of space between the attendees and the musicians.

Only these attendees generally had their backs to the Raver, or slighting angled away to give the appearance of indifference while also keeping the Raver in their peripheral vision.

The women kept watch — subtly. The men? Backs fully turned.

My calculations came to this:

I could not step from the curb to walk my way past the Raver, or that would indicate too strongly my deference to him.

Those who know, know this would alert him and allow him, if he was so inclined, to select a target, namely me.

Too much scrutiny, it seems, begets scrutiny.

So while I could not step from the curb, I could ease my way
to the very edge around the surrounding crowd and progress
forward. My ideal would be behind but as we've stated before, that
wasn't a possibility.

Furthermore, the road the sidewalk accompanied was about 4.
Lanes of traffic deep and the cars which traversed it, though not
magnitudinous, were mostly hightailing at un-side-street-like
speeds.

Therefore I had the option to be hit by a speeding car or pass
uncomfortably near the Raver.

There didn't seem to be much of an option.

So I sidled inconspicuously as far from the Raver as possible
(having not interrupted a single stride throughout my deliberation)
while staying staunchly on the sidewalk.

I eased my way past the other bus-takers and as I passed
the Raver un-harassed and unharmed, I released a barely

perceptible sigh of relief.

Yet another incident avoided, yet another over-complicated, over-anxious over-analysis, I told myself.

Well, I thought placatingly, maybe so but I haven't been mugged or assaulted yet, so I can't really fault myself for my overabundance of caution, can I?

And just at that moment, from behind, the Raver grabbed my shoulder.

Adrenaline.

Fear.

Rage.

No thought, just action.

I ripped my shoulder from his grasp and whipped around.

My finger up, at the ready...

"DONTCHU…" I hissed menacingly.

Frankly, I don't know what I was going to say but I felt a mushed

up version of a "Don't You" come growling out of me.

I stared him down and he stopped, utterly still.

We stood.

Standing.

Staring.

Opposite one another.

My teeth bared, my finger gunned.

Him, arms limp at his side, eyes unwavering.

I couldn't finish whatever words I'd intended to say, nothing

left just… a dare, maybe?

As in, 'Don't you dare… or even… Don't touch me, I dare you to try…

Both possible. I couldn't tell you myself.

I felt it when he released.

The moment he… acquiesced … conceded.

I won. I knew it.

Whenever I regale someone with this story (which is admittedly rare) I like to say that his crazy met mine and he knew which was worse.

There was another time a young woman told me about.

At a large mall, a denizen of trash and myopic mementos of plastic and apathy; excepting of course the indoor amusement park — I'm the only one I know who has hit a barrel roll at least twice on the mean green ride.

Where were we?

Ah, yes

The mall.

The young woman said there was a man.

And with the man was a woman.

And that man 'aggressed' that woman.

Right outside her store.

She said they'd called security but that they never showed up.

The woman was cowed and dejected.

The crowd.

The useless onlookers who let it happen.

I wonder sometimes what I would have done, back then, in that scenario.

I truly believe it would depend on the day as well as my attire.

It's hard to throw a punch in a waist trainer.

Trust me. I know from experience.

Not to mention the delivery isn't as forceful when you're constricted from the crucial movement meant to deliver the biggest impact.

Anywho, I remember telling that woman: I wish.

As in, I wish someone tried that near me.

And I continued: I've been waiting for that moment.

As in, I have a lot of pent up rage and day to day interactions don't usually warrant enough violence to release it all in a socially acceptable manner.

I'd wished for violence.

Yearned for it.

I think back on that conversation not infrequently.

While I am very good at what I do, I guess the saying rings true:

Be careful what you wish for.

Bergslagen

The girl buried it.

Her sorrow knew no bounds

But she'd been left with no choice

For the past 9 months she'd wept in every dark staircase and every cold shower.

There were no places you could leave it

It would be eaten by wolves or worse

They watched

She'd let it happen she told herself

When she thought back to that traumatic moment

She'd made a split second decision

One meant to preserve her sanity

Fight.

Struggle.

Scream.

Make it worse.

Make it exponentially worse.

Or

Submit

Depart

Stay quiet

Wait for it to be over.

Then be done with it.

Better to acquiesce quietly

The screaming wouldn't stop it.

Wouldn't make it go away

So

To make it better for herself

To ease her mind

To prevent more violence

Better to leave that moment bruised in one place than all the others

She made her choice

She didn't have a chance to think on the future

She didn't even really believe it could happen

A commemoration

It shouldn't be possible

So many people beg for it

So many suffer the lack of it

Unwanted. Unwilling. Unready. Unripe

She did all the things one isn't supposed to do.

But it stuck

And it grew

So she lied. And she hid.

And she wept

And then...

she buried it.

She buried it in a special place

A place made hollow by other bodies

Under a large weeping willow

She didn't want it to be lonely

She didn't want it to get wet

There were no other options

Her mother was not a forgiving mother

And no excuses or truths would be believed

She would be without a home, without a job, without any capability
to care for herself, much less

another being

Another breathing, thinking, feeding being.

They would both die.

A horrible death

This, she reasoned, was the one awful thing she was allowed

She could emerge… not better, no… but at least not hopeless.

She didn't account for the dreams

It's face

Haunting

The rest of her miserable life would be short and even more miserable with it.

Without it, it loomed long ahead of her.

An… attachment

Time, she assumed, might make the problem go away

But after the dreams, came the cries

                              The wails

She stopped sleeping, her eyes bloodshot

                  Her skin sallow

Her cheeks sunken

                    She became a shell

        Her parents, concerned, brought her to specialists.

They helped, a little.

A year later her father was working near the place of the dead.

        He leaned against the bark of the old willow

He leaned and he lit a cigarette

A small child appeared

As if, from nowhere

Barely able to walk

Barely able to talk

"May I?"

The old man squinted through the smoke

"Ask your mother, child, and leave me be," the old man
responded.

And with that, the child left.

Almost as if in smoke.

The girl lay in bed.

Where she'd been the whole year

She heard a noise

Not a wail

But a giggle.

Too exhausted to care, she fell back asleep before she could feel fear.

The bed dipped under a weight

She cracked an eye open

"Mother," it wheezed

The first year of the first born

"Mother."

She let out a gasp of terror

But her arms opened of their own volition

"Child," she rasped

And now, they walk

Hand in hand

Through the valley there

It, ever wailing

Her, ever weeping

Together forever

They walk.

No Words

D octor Mischelvi was not a man to take things lightly.

One of the things the Doctor hated the most was being boxed in or ... constricted.

He had, at one time in a totally freak accident, been locked in a truck for almost three days and barely survived.

You could say he was claustrophobic, but obviously not within his hearing.

Or at least not until the breakthrough

The Doctor had very strong convictions. Specifically, he thought that his incapacity to empathize with other humans was a direct result of the barrier of language.

Of course, he spoke English like any one else in his vicinity

But of course, being the savant he is, he has a hard time making himself understood.

It bothered him.

And what happens when a genius is bothered by something?

Something well within their capability of fixing?

Or better yet, a problem that remains to be solved which, though troublesome, is not futile.

In his word, "Language is an inhibition. It… blocks us in. We are blocked by what we say and how we describe things… it is limiting beyond bounds."

The lack of access to comprehension has, (in his words) prevented more art, more scientific breakthroughs, more utopian existences.

We are held back by our inability to form coherent sentences.

That they are coherent to us innately but not to others is a clear example of such a thing.

Ideas form around language, the ideas are bound by their limits.

The limitations prevent possibilities.

Language is a puzzle, and only one or two puzzle masters exist within an eon. We've already used up ours with Shakespeare.

[During this part of his diatribe, he, usually standing proud upon the dias, pauses for effect, a little light laughter from the audience, perhaps; they usually oblige]

His solution

Elegant

    Of course

        What would you expect of the dear doctor

Telepathy

    Mindreading

      Initially, he thought of a microchip embedded in the brain

A small, minimally invasive surgery; barely any down time.

          But the problem would be the adoption
rates.

    While he understood his breakthrough to be world altering in
and of itself, the brain chip wasn't sufficiently marketable for the
purposes he would like to derive from his work.

He wanted to be able to communicate with anyone

            Barriers lifted

Reduction of constriction, remember?

So he went back to work.

It took him ten years of research

Probably more than one set of clandestine human trials

No one was ever really able to tell him no.

He just wouldn't allow it

When it finally came, it was preposterous

Some sort of chemical rebalancing, delivered via radio wave

Something in the tissue damaged in a particular way reworked

electrical pathways causing... solvency

To be honest, even with telepathy, I still can't comprehend it.

The problem was...

The aftermath

From one second to another.

Millions died.

Self mutilation. Mass suicides. Mass homicide.

He was alarmed, to say the least.

But the process is not reversible.

So, no one knew the real reason for the deliverance into this new world until recently.

And of course, as it does, the news spreads like wildfire.

But, as it does (it took ages for us to learn this) the news can be… misleading

If you've ever played the game of telephone you'd probably think this was a no brainer.

But when you're hearing it with all the conviction one possesses through the mind of a telepathic…

It's hard to disbelieve.

Especially those untrained

The sudden drop in population was destabilizing for the entire globe.

It required a lot of people getting together and committing to each other

There were many failed attempts

Just because you understand doesn't mean you have to agree.

It seems the folks who generally used to become politicians usually became those for purposes other than honesty and constituent interest.

People had to be foisted into the roles by a quorum

Those who didn't want it were, unsurprisingly, the best at the job.

Now that the wars are over, the mass starvation and attacks

have mostly dissipated.

We all agree we're very much better off.

It's still challenging to be interrupted by the thought patterns of a grotesque.

They're usually already delivered to restricted areas and left to fend for themselves. Their survival rates are very low, but some make it through.

My work, introducing the good doctor to the rest of the world, has resulted in some dubious responses but the majority of recipients are overjoyed to have an answer at last.

The overmasters, the religious organizations which sprouted up under the belief that the "gift' was delivered by the means of a deity… we have to watch out for them. Most of them have had their mouths sewn shut in solidarity with their religious views so they're not often difficult to spot.

He's had fewer than 100 assassination attempts. So I think we've done a great job.

We're all very happy to have him.

We've asked him to begin research on further expansions of human capacity.

We cannot wait to see what he comes up with next.

Black and White and Blue

The girl on the train had never seen the man before.

He wore a black and white diamond-checkered suit.

The girl fingered the box.

Her mother had given her that box before she went away.

The girl always had the box with her. She took it on the train every day.

It had been worn smooth on the sides where she tended to run her hands over it whenever she felt anxious or excited.

That morning, her grandmother had told her to take an umbrella.

There was no rain in the forecast, and the sky was clear.

But when Grandmother asked, you listened.

You listened because of the time you didn't — and broke your femur.

You listened because of the time you didn't — and got a concussion.

You listened because of the time when Sally got into that accident and there was brain fluid leaking from her ears.

So the girl had her box. And she had her umbrella.

Oddly enough, the black-and-white-suited man had one too.

They looked at one another across the train...

Evaluating

There was one thing the girl hadn't listened to her grandmother about.

And that was the box.

The box was from her mother.

Nothing could take the box away from the girl. Nothing.

The black-and-white-suited man moved to sit next to her.

"Tip Top Trouble O'Clock," he said, looking at her expectantly.

"Excuse me?" She asked.

Then she remembered

This morning while Grandmother was making breakfast and the girl had been in the shower.

Grandmother had shouted something … something that just now sounded like: "Give help to black and white."

The girl sucked her teeth.

Grandmother

Her eyes narrowed.

The man talked animatedly. He seemed to like her immediately.

He asked to see her box.

She considered denying his request, but remembered her grandmother's enticement.

She handed it over, reluctantly, describing it to him, sharing some of its history.

The man nosed about and responded, "Yes, and before that, it was a prison."

She looks at him sharply, "a what?"

For the night terrors, of course," he scoffed.

He examined her closely. "You didn't know?"

He chuckled to himself, pressed a few spots jovially—

and the box opened.

She hadn't known the box could open.

They both looked inside. The man inhaled sharply, "IT'S NOT EMPTY!"

He chucked the box away like it was scalding and grabbed her hand, dragging her down the train corridor.

Barely keeping up, she tried to free herself to go back for it.

A loud crash sounded behind her. She glanced back.

A black, tentacled monster was tearing through the train – eating, destroying, throbbing its way toward them faster

than it should have been able to move.

The girl screeched and put on the thrusters.

She nearly passed the man in the black and white suit, "Why'd you let me open it if it WASN'T EMPTY?!" he shouts.

"I didn't even know it could OPEN, YOU IDIOT!" she yelled back, breathless.

The cacophony of screams and crunching behind them built to a crescendo.

The monster, for its part, hated the girl. It hated her with every fiber of its being.

From inside its prison, it had watched the world through her. Every second of every day.

Through her eyes.

Every day, her face. Every day, her hands.

It knew her more intimately than a sibling.

And it had waited.

She would not escape the misery it had planned for her after all these long years.

The man threw her into an alcove and quickly propped a mirror against the exterior door.

He positioned her, and held her tightly against him.

The creature stormed past them—straight into the mirror—and off the train.

It tumbled onto the tracks. Black ichor sprayed the entire back side of the train.

The man yelled in triumph, "That was the quickest thinking I've done in quite a while!

His grin spreads from ear to ear.

Then they feel it.

The train begins to slow.

They were arriving at the next stop.

This is the girls stop.

The man's grin vanished.

He grabbed her hand and they ran.

Metal screamed behind them. The girl looked back—

more monsters poured from the car with the opened box.

"There are MORE of them?!" she screamed in horror.

The man twisted around, screeching, "THERE ARE MORE OF THEM!?"

She let out an exasperated noise and steered them toward her house.

Halfway there, her grandmother appeared, hobbling quickly on her cane.

When she saw them, she waved her cane wildly, shouting, "I told you I never liked that damn box!"

A monster flanked them — pouring out from an alley near the building beside her grandmother.

The girl shrieked.

Her grandmother spun, cane pointed like a spear, and shouted words the girl couldn't hear.

A pale blue light streaked from the cane, striking the monster in the chest.

It made a terrible sound as it burned from the inside out.

Another, bigger monster rose behind it – angry for its brother.

It charged toward her grandmother.

The girl and the man were nearly there — but not fast enough.

The man released her hand.

"MORIBUS!" he shouted, and the creature was blasted back a few feet.

But only a few.

It whipped its tail and slammed him across the street. The girl barely dodged in time.

Knowing she was running to her death, the girl squared her stance.

She didn't know if it would work.

Didn't care.

She threw her hands toward the monster.

"Moribus!" she screamed.

The blast knocked her backward. She hit the pavement and blacked out.

When she came to, the man in the black and white suit was now half blue.

One side of his suit remained black and white. The other, fully blue.

He helped her grandmother to her feet.

Together, they approached the girl.

As he neared, she saw that his face had turned blue too.

"We've got a lot of work to do," he tells her seriously, brushing dust from her coat.

The Specialist

I watch him from his pulpit

From the sidelines

I've been with him, by his side for a long time now

He's a connoisseur

A savant

He's tried and tested every faith there is

Every. Single. One.

And here's the rub… he's truly tried it

He's lived it, breathed it, read it, existed in it

And then one day, years, months later... he's done

He's ready

He's achieved something

So he moves on

I've never known what it was, what the trigger is that prompts him

to begin anew

Any hour, any moment

And the Faiths. The Faiths

From my perspective, as an outsider, I see the differences ... and

the similarities

Some religions have more pigheadedness than others

Some, flimsiness

But all, all have basic tenets

Basis rules

It's as if every founder of every religion was bound by the same narrow corridors in their minds.

And every thing they could possibly conceive of

Every basic structure

A road already traveled

A course already plotted

The details change, of course

But, the meat... the framework... at its very heart

Duplicative.

And he knows this

And so he's come to this

I saw it

The beginning

And I did not know it for what it was

In the midst of prayer

The switch flipped

He stood up and began collecting his belongings

Another man spoke in rebuke

He turned

He spoke

He provoked

The crowd surged

He challenged them

"Take this, your belief"

"Do you dare test your faith?"

"Do you dare?"

A challenge issued

"You who claim to be true followers."

"Prove yourselves."

And so it went

And in that precious moment

A reed

A wind

Any which way

But the reed broke

And in its place, a new theology

A changed theology

I've never seen anything like it

No one has

And its spread

Like a virus

Like a plague

I don't think he planned this from the beginning

I think... in his search... he found something within himself

Something ... other

Maybe his studies, his bodies work has rewired him

Made him into this

Maybe it was a hole, a wound, open for too long

And him, the healing salve

The connection, the disconnection

                              Maybe that's what drove him

A compulsion to fix. To serve. To understand

Well… I can't speak to his understanding, I don't have that range.

                    But

              I see it

                    In him

What the others lacked

                              He has created

And all are drawn to it

                         A new world dawns

Mirrorball

In the bustling town of Violetville, lived many a bustling citizen

All were industrious, though some more well-heeled than others

Now, the town had a curfew.

But few paid attention to it

You most assuredly did not want to be caught out

So ways were made – trails to keep these bustling citizens

working through the wee hours of the night

On this particular night, two such citizens were out and about

One, a gentleman

His occupation: watermelon juice maker

Watson, his name, spent most days at the market

He always carried at least one watermelon on his person--just in case

In an emergency, he could pierce a melon and pour juice for a fraction of his competitors' prices in a fraction of the time

He was rarely caught unprepared

He planned too well for that

The second traveler was a woman

An heiress in fact

To a mirror mine

Because of her family's prime export, she was required to carry

no fewer than four mirrors at all times

Not to sell, like the juice-maker.

To perform

To display

To showcase the glory and shine the mirrors bestowed

In truth, she didn't care for them. She never used them

Like many young heirs, she felt a moral obligation to dislike what

had made her rich

Still, she carried her mirrors that night — fourteen of them, in

accordance with expectation

Each traveler took their own secret path — dark stairwells beneath

the town

Each had their own purpose

                                                  Neither saw the other

As was custom, they wore dark clothing past curfew

And, in their hurry

                They crashed

                        They tumbled

                                They fell

Clutching one another, they waited for the end

When they hit bottom, they landed with a splat, lying flat on their

backs

And there — suspended from an outstretched branch of a

                    long-dead tree — hung the melon

But no, not simply the melon

The mirrors

A mirror, lodged deep inside the fruit, twinkled with fractured

light

Shards glimmered

It swayed, back and forth, catching the moon

The two citizens stood and brushed each other off

She saw a glint of light caught in the blue of his eyes

He saw another rebound off the red-gold shine of her hair

They looked up in unison

Back and forth, the mirrorball swayed

Watson offered his hand

And they began to dance a waltz

Hours, they dance

Isabella Falconeri

The light dances with them

The next evening, they married

The morning after, they filed the patent

And the rest, as they say, is history

Thank You for Reading

Stories don't end on the page — they echo in the quiet places they leave behind.

In the Mountain's Shadow was born of questions: what we endure, what we sacrifice, and the fragile threads that bind us to one another.

If these pages moved you, I would be honored if you shared a brief review on Amazon or Goodreads. Your words help others find their way here — and help keep this story alive.

Until we meet again, in the spaces between stories

— Isabella Falconeri

Made in the USA
Monee, IL
01 December 2025